RED BLADES OF BLACK CATHAY

BY

ROBERT E. HOWARD

British Library Cataloguing-in-Publication Data
A catalogue record for this book is available from the
British Library

Contents

Contents

Robert E. Howard

Robert Ervin Howard was born in Peaster, Texas in 1906. During his youth, his family moved between a variety of Texan boomtowns, and Howard – a bookish and somewhat introverted child – was steeped in the violent myths and legends of the Old South. Although he loved reading and learning, Howard developed a distinctly Texan, hardboiled outlook on the world. He became a passionate fan of boxing, taking it up at an amateur level, and from the age of nine began to write adventure tales of semi-historical bloodshed. In 1919, when Howard was thirteen, his family moved to the Central Texas hamlet of Cross Plains, where he would stay for the rest of his life.

At fifteen Howard began to read the pulp magazines of the day, and to write more seriously. The December 1922 issue of his high school newspaper featured two of his stories, 'Golden Hope Christmas' and 'West is West'. In 1924 he sold his first piece – a short caveman tale titled 'Spear and Fang' – for $16 to the not-yet-famous *Weird Tales* magazine. He published with the magazine regularly over the next few years. 1929 was a breakout year for Howard, in that the 23-year-old writer began to sell to other magazines, such as *Ghost Stories* and *Argosy*, both of whom had previously sent him hundreds of rejection slips. In 1930, he began a correspondence with weird fiction master H. P. Lovecraft which ran up to his death six years later, and is regarded as one of the great correspondence cycles in all of fantasy literature.

It was partly due to Lovecraft's encouragement that Howard created his most famous character, Conan the Cimmerian. Conan – a barbarian-turned-King during the Hyborian Age, a mythical period of some 12,000 years ago – featured in seventeen *Weird Tales* stories between 1933 and 1936, and is now regarded as having spawned the 'sword and sorcery' genre, making Howard's influence on fantasy literature comparable to that of J. R. R. Tolkien's. The Conan stories have since been adapted many times, most famously in the series of films starring Arnold Schwarzenegger.

Howard was enjoying an all-time high in sales by the beginning of 1936, but he was also deeply upset by the ill health of his mother, who had fallen into a coma. On the morning of June 11, 1936, he asked an attending nurse whether she would ever recover, and the nurse replied negatively. Howard walked to his car, parked outside the family home in Cross Plains, and shot himself. He died eight hours later, aged just thirty.

Trumpets die in the loud parade,
The gray mist drinks the spears;
Banners of glory sink and fade
In the dust of a thousand years.
Singers of pride the silence stills,
The ghost of empire goes,
But a song still lives in the ancient hills,
And the scent of a vanished rose.
Ride with us on a dim, lost road
To the dawn of a distant day,
When swords were bare for a guerdon rare --

''The Flower of Black Cathay.''

CHAPTER I

The singing of the swords was a deathly clamor in the brain of Godric de Villehard. Blood and sweat veiled his eyes and in the instant of blindness he felt a keen point pierce a joint of his hauberk and sting deep into his ribs. Smiting blindly, he felt the jarring impact that meant his sword had gone home, and snatching an instant's grace, he flung back his vizor and wiped the redness from his eyes. A single glance only was allowed him: in that glance he had a fleeting glimpse of huge, wild black mountains; of a clump of mail-clad warriors, ringed by a howling horde of human wolves; and in the center of that clump, a slim, silk-clad shape standing between a dying horse and a dying swordsman. Then the wolfish figures surged in on all sides, hacking like madmen.

"Christ and the Cross!" the old Crusading shout rose in a ghastly croak from Godric's parched lips. As if far away he heard voices gaspingly repeat the words. Curved sabers rained on shield and helmet. Godric's eyes blurred to the sweep of frenzied dark faces with bristling, foam-flecked beards. He fought like a man in a dream. A great weariness fettered his limbs. Somewhere -- long ago it seemed -- a heavy axe, shattering on his helm, had bitten through an old dent to rend the scalp beneath. He heaved his curiously weighted arm above his head and split a bearded face to the chin.

"*En avant*, Montferrat!" We must hack through and shatter the gates, thought the dazed brain of Godric; we can not long stand this press, but once within the city -- no -- these walls were not the walls of Constantinople: he was mad; he dreamed -- these towering heights were the crags of a lost and nameless land and Montferrat and the Crusade lay lost in leagues and years.

Godric's steed reared and pitched headlong, throwing his rider with a clash of armor. Under the lashing hoofs and the shower of blades, the knight struggled clear and rose, without his shield, blood starting from every joint in his armor. He reeled, bracing himself; he fought not these foes alone, but the long grinding days behind -- the days and days of hard riding and ceaseless fighting.

Godric thrust upward and a man died. A scimitar shivered on his crest, and the wielder, torn from his saddle by a hand that was still iron, spilled his entrails at Godric's feet. The rest reined in around howling, seeking to overthrow the giant Frank by sheer weight of numbers. Somewhere in the hellish din a woman's scream knifed the air. A clatter of hoofs burst like a sudden whirlwind and the press was cleared. Through a red mist the dulling eyes of the knight saw the wolfish, skin-clad assailants swept away by a sudden flood of mailed riders who hacked them down and trampled them under.

Then men were dismounting around him, men whose gaudy silvered armor, high fur kaftans and two-handed scimitars he saw as in a dream. One with thin drooping mustaches adorning his dark face spoke to him in a Turkish tongue the knight could faintly understand, but the burden of the words was unintelligible. He shook his head.

"I can not linger," Godric said, speaking slowly and with growing difficulty, "De Montferrat awaits my report and I must -- ride -- East -- to -- find -- the -- kingdom -- of -- Prester -- John -- bid -- my -- men -- mount -- "

His voice trailed off. He saw his men; they lay about in a silent, sword-gashed cluster, dead as they had lived -- facing the foe. Suddenly the strength flowed from Godric de Villehard in a great surge and he fell as a blasted tree falls. The red mist closed about him, but ere it engulfed him utterly, he saw bending near him two great dark eyes, strangely soft and luminous, that filled him with formless yearning; in a world grown dim and unreal they were the one tangible reality and this vision he took with him into a nightmare realm of shadows.

Godric's return to waking life was as abrupt as his departure. He opened his eyes to a scene of exotic splendor. He was lying on a silken couch near a wide window whose sill and bars were of chased gold. Silken cushions littered the marble floor and the walls were of mosaics where they were not worked in designs of gems and silver, and were hung with heavy tapestries of silk, satin and cloth-of-gold. The ceiling was a single lofty dome of lapis lazuli from which was suspended on golden chains a censer that shed a faint alluring scent over all. Through the window a faint breeze wafted scents of spices, roses and jasmine, and beyond Godric could see the clear blue of the Asian skies.

He tried to rise and fell back with a startled exclamation. Whence this strange weakness? The hand he lifted to his gaze was thinner than should be, and its bronze was faded. He gazed in perplexity at the silken, almost feminine garments which clothed him, and then he remembered -- the long wandering, the battle, the slaughter of his men-at-arms. His heart turned sick within him as he remembered the staunch faithfulness of the men he had led to the shambles.

A tall, thin yellow man with a kindly face entered and smiled to see that he was awake and in his right mind. He spoke to the knight in several languages unknown to Godric, then used one easy to understand -- a rough Turkish dialect much akin to the bastard tongue used by the Franks in their contacts with the Turanian peoples.

"What place is this?" asked Godric. "How long have I lain here?"

"You have lain here many days," answered the other. "I am You-tai, the emperor's man-of-healing. This is the heaven-born empire of Black Cathay. The princess Yulita has attended you with her own hands while you lay raving in delirium. Only through her care and your own marvelous natural strength have you survived. When she told the emperor how you with your small band recklessly charged and delivered her from the hands of the Hian bandits who had slain her guard and taken her prisoner, the heavenly one gave command that naught be spared to preserve you. Who are you, most noble lord? While you raved you spoke of many unknown peoples, places and battles and your appearance is such as to show that you come from afar."

Godric laughed, and bitterness was in his laughter.

"Aye," quoth he, "I have ridden far; the deserts have parched my lips and the mountains have wearied my feet. I have seen Trebizond in my wanderings, and Teheran and Bokhara and Samarcand. I have looked on the waters of the Black Sea and the Sea of Ravens. From Constantinople far to the west I set forth more than a year agone, riding eastward. I am a knight of Normandy, Sir Godric de Villehard."

"I have heard of some of the places you name," answered You-tai, "but many of them are unknown to me. Eat now, and rest. In time the princess Yulita will come to you."

So Godric ate the curiously spiced rice, the dates and candied meats, and drank the colorless rice wine brought him by a flat-faced girl slave who wore golden bangles on her ankles, and soon slept, and sleeping, his unquenchable vitality began to assert itself.

When he awoke from that long sleep he felt refreshed and stronger, and soon the pearl-inlaid doors opened and a slight, silk-clad figure entered. Godric's heart suddenly pounded as he again felt the soft, tender gaze of those great dark eyes upon him. He drew himself together with an effort; was he a boy to tremble before a pair of eyes, even though they adorned the face of a princess?

Long used was he to the veiled women of the Moslems, and Yulita's creamy cheeks with her full ruby lips were like an oasis in the waste.

"I am Yulita," the voice was soft, vibrant and musical as the silvery tinkle of the fountain in the court outside. "I wish to thank you. You are brave as Rustum. When the Hians rushed from the defiles and cut down my guard, I was afraid. You answered my screams as unexpectedly and boldly as a hero sent down from paradise. I am sorry your brave men died."

"And I likewise," the Norman answered with the bluntness of his race, "but it was their trade: they would not have had it otherwise and they could not have died in a better cause."

"But why did you risk your life to aid me, who am not of your race and whom you never saw before?" she pursued.

Godric might have answered as would nine out of any ten knights in his position -- with the repeating of the vow of chivalry, to protect all weaker things. But being Godric de Villehard, he shrugged his shoulders. "God knows. I should have known it was death to us all to charge that horde. I have seen too much rapine and outrage since I turned my face east to have thus thrown away my men and expedition in the ordinary course of events. Perhaps I saw at a glance you were of regal blood and followed the knight's natural instinct to rush to the aid of royalty."

She bowed her head. "I am sorry."

"I am not," he growled. "My men would have died anyhow today or tomorrow -- now they are at rest. We have ridden through hell for more than a year. Now they are beyond the sun's heat and the Turk's saber." She rested her chin on her hands and her elbows on her knees, leaning forward to gaze deep into his eyes. His senses swam momentarily. Her eyes traversed his mighty frame to return to his face. Thin-lipped, with cold gray eyes, Godric de Villehard's sun-darkened, clean-shaven face inspired trust and respect in men but there was little in his appearance to stir the heart of a woman. The Norman was not past thirty, but his hard life had carved his face into inflexible lines. Rather than the beauty that appeals to women, there was in his features the lean strength of the hunting wolf. The forehead was high and broad, the brow of a thinker, and once the mouth had been kindly, the eyes those of a dreamer. But now his eyes were bitter and his whole appearance that of a man with whom life has dealt hardly -- who has ceased to look for mercy or to give it.

"Tell me, Sir Godric," said Yulita, "whence come you and why have you ridden so far with so few men?"

"It's a long tale," he answered. "It had its birth in a land halfway across the world. I was a boy and full of high ideals of chivalry and knighthood -- and I hated that Saxon-French pig, King John. A wine-bibber named Fulk of Neuilly began ranting and screaming death and damnation because the Holy Land was still in the possession of the Paynim. He howled until he stirred the blood of such young fools as myself, and the barons began recruiting men -- forgetting how the other Crusades had ended.

"Walter de Brienne and that black-faced cut-throat Simon de Montfort fired us young Normans with promises of salvation and Turkish loot, and we set forth. Boniface and Baldwin were our leaders and they plotted against each other all the way to Venice.

"There the mercenary Venetians refused us ships and it sickened my very entrails to see our chiefs go down on their knees to those merchant swine. They promised us ships at last but they set such a high price we could not pay. None of us had any money, else we had never started on that mad venture. We wrenched the jewels from our hilts and the gold from our buckles and raised part of the money, bargaining to take various cities from the Greeks and give them over to Venice for the rest of the price. The Pope -- Innocent III -- raged, but we went our ways and quenched our swords in Christian blood instead of Paynim.

"Spalato we took, and Ragusa, Sebenico and Zara. The Venetians got the cities and we got the glory." Here Godric laughed harshly. A quick glance told him the girl was sitting spellbound, eyes aglow. Somehow he felt ashamed.

"Well," he continued, "young Alexius who had been driven from Constantinople persuaded us that it would be doing God's work to put old Angelus back on the throne, so we fared forth.

"We took Constantinople with no great difficulty, but only a scant time had elapsed before the maddened people strangled old Angelus and we were forced to take the city again. This time we sacked it and split the empire up. De Montfort had long returned to England and I fought under Boniface of Montferrat, who was made King of Macedonia. One day he called me to him, and said he: 'Godric, the Turkomans harry the caravans and the trade of the East dries up because of constant war. Take a hundred men-at-arms and find me this kingdom of Prester John. He too is a Christian and we may establish a route of trade between us, guarded by both of us, and thus safeguard the caravans.'

"Thus he spoke, being a natural-born liar and unable to tell the truth on a wager. I saw through his design and understood his wish for me to conquer this fabulous kingdom for him.

"'Only a hundred men?' quoth I.

"'I can not spare you more,' said he, 'lest Baldwin and Dandolo and the Count of Blois come in and cut my throat. These are enow. Gain ye to Prester John and abide with him awhile -- aid him in his wars for a space, then send riders to report your progress to me. Mayhap then I can send you more men.' And his eyelids drooped in a way I knew. "'But where lies this kingdom?' said I.

"'Easy enough,' said he; 'to the east -- any fool can find it if he fares far enough.'

"So," Godric's face darkened, "I rode east with a hundred heavily armed horsemen -- the pick of the Norman warriors. By Satan, we hacked our way through! Once past Trebizond we had to fight almost every mile. We were assailed by Turks, Persians and Kirghiz, as well as by our natural foes of heat, thirst and hunger. A hundred men -- there were less than a score with me when I heard your screams and rode out of the defiles. Their bodies lie scattered from the hills of Black Cathay to the shores of the Black Sea. Arrows, spears, swords, all took their toll, but still I forged eastward."

"And all for your liege lord!" cried Yulita, her eyes sparkling, as she clasped her hands. "Oh, it is like the tales of honor and chivalry; of Iran and those You-tai has told me of the heroes of ancient Cathay. It makes my blood burn! You too are a hero such as all men were once in the days of our ancestors, with your courage and loyalty!"

The sting of his healing wounds bit into Godric.

"Loyalty?" he snarled. "To that devious-minded assassin, Montferrat? Bah! Do you think I intended giving up my life to carve out a kingdom for him? He had naught to lose and all to gain. He gave me a handful of men, expecting to receive the rewards of what I did. If I failed, he was still winner, for he would be rid of a turbulent vassal. The kingdom of Prester John is a dream and a fantasy. I have followed a will-o'-the-wisp for a thousand miles. A dream that receded farther and farther into the mazes of the East, leading me to my doom."

"And had you found it, what then?" asked the girl, grown suddenly quiet.

Godric shrugged his shoulders. It was not the Norman way to flaunt secret ambitions to any chance-met man or woman, but after all, he owed his life to this girl. She had paid her debt to him and there was something in her eyes....

"Had I found Prester John's kingdom," said Godric, "I had made shift to conquer it for myself."

"Look," Yulita took Godric's arm and pointed out a gold-barred window, whose sheer silken curtains, blowing inward, disclosed the rugged peaks of distant mountains, shouldering against the blazing blue of the skies.

"Beyond those mountains lies the kingdom of him you call Prester John."

Godric's eyes gleamed suddenly with the conquering spirit of the true Norman -- the born empire-maker, whose race had carved out kingdoms with their swords in every land of the West and Near East.

"And does he dwell in purple-domed palaces of gold and glittering gems?" he asked eagerly. "Do, as I have heard, learned philosophers and magi sit at either hand, doing wonders with stars and suns and ghosts of the mighty dead? Does his city loom among the clouds with golden spires thrusting among the stars? And does the deathless monarch, who learned at the feet of our fair Lord Christ, sit on an ivory throne in a room whose walls are carved of one great sapphire dispensing justice?"

She shook her head.

"Prester John -- Wang Khan we name him -- is very old, but he is not deathless nor has he ever been beyond the confines of his own kingdom. His people are the Keraits -- Krits -- Christians; they dwell in cities, true, but the houses are mud huts and goatskin tents, and the palace of Wang Khan is as a hut itself compared to this palace." Godric fell back and his eyes went dull.

"My dream is vanished," he muttered. "You should have let me die."

"Dream again, man," she answered; "only dream something more attainable."

Shaking his head, he looked into her eyes.

"Dreams of empire have haunted my life," said he, "yet even now the shadow of a dream lingers in my soul, ten times less attainable than the kingdom of Prester John."

CHAPTER II

"Scrawled screens and secret gardens
And insect-laden skies --
Where fiery plains stretch on and on
To the purple country of Prester John
And the walls of Paradise."

-- Chesterton

The days passed and slowly the giant frame of the Norman knight regained its accustomed vigor. In those days he sat in the chamber with the lapis lazuli dome, or walked in the outer courts where fountains tinkled musically beneath the shade of cherry trees, and soft petals fell in a colorful rain about him. The battle-scarred warrior felt strangely out of place in this setting of exotic luxury but was inclined to rest there and lull the restlessness of his nature for a time. He saw nothing of the city, Jahadur, for the walls about the courts were high, and he presently understood that he was practically a prisoner. He saw only Yulita, the slaves and You-tai. With the thin yellow man he talked much. You-tai was a Cathayan -- a member of the race who lived in Greater Cathay, some distance to the south. This empire, Godric soon realized, had given rise to many of the tales of Prester

18

John; it was an ancient, mighty but now loosely knit empire, divided into three kingdoms -- the Khitai, the Chin and the Sung. You-tai was learned beyond any man Godric had ever known and he spoke freely.

"The emperor inquires often after your health," said he, "but I tell you frankly, it were best that you not be presented to him for a time at least. Since your great battle with the Hian bandits, you have captured the fancy of the soldiers, especially old Roogla, the general who loves the princess like his own since he bore her as a babe on his saddle-bow from the ruins of Than when the Naimans raided over the border. Chamu Khan fears anyone the army loves. He fears you might be a spy. He fears most things, does the emperor, even his niece, the princess Yulita."

"She does not took like the Black Cathayan girls I have seen" commented Godric; "her face is not flat, nor do her eyes slant as much."

"She has Iranian blood," answered You-tai. "She is the daughter of a royal Black Cathayan and a Persian woman."

"I see sadness in her eyes, at times," said Godric.

"She remembers that she is soon to leave her mountain home," answered You-tai, eyeing Godric closely. "She is to marry prince Wang Yin of the Chin emperors. Chamu Khan has promised her to him, for he is anxious to gain favor with Cathay. The emperor fears Genghis Khan."

"Who is Genghis Khan?" Godric asked idly.

"A chief of the Yakka Mongols. He has grown greatly in power for the last decade. His people are nomads -- fierce fighters who have so little to live for in their barren deserts that they do not mind dying. Long ago their ancestors, the Hiong-nu, were driven into the Gobi by my ancestors, the Cathayans. They are divided into many tribes and fight against one another, but Genghis Khan seems to be uniting them by conquest. I even hear wild tales that he plans to shake off the liege-ship of Cathay and even make war on his masters. But that is foolish. This small kingdom is different. Though Hia and the Keraits lie between Chamu Khan and the Yakkas, Genghis Khan is a real threat to this mountain empire.

"Black Cathay has grown to be a kingdom apart, pent in the fastness where no strong foe has come against them for ages. They are neither Turks nor Chinese any longer, but constitute a separate nation of their own, with separate traditions. They have never needed any alliances for protection, but now since they have grown soft and degenerate from long years of peace, even Chamu realizes their weaknesses and seeks to ally his house with that of the Chins of Cathay."

Godric mused a space. "It would seem Jahadur is the key to Black Cathay. These Mongols must first take this city to make sure of their conquests. No doubt the walls throng with archers and spearmen?"

You-tai spread his hands helplessly. "No man knows the mind of Chamu Khan. There are scarce fifteen hundred warriors in the city. Chamu has even sent our strongest detachment -- a troop of hard-riding western Turks -- to another part of the empire. Why, no one knows. I beg you, stir not from the court until I tell you. Chamu Khan deems you a spy of Genghis Khan, I fear, and it were best if he did not send for you."

But Chamu Khan did call for Godric before many days had drifted by. The emperor gave him audience, not in the great throne room, but in a small chamber where Chamu Khan squatted like a great fat toad on a silken divan attended by a huge black mute with a two-handed scimitar. Godric veiled the contempt in his eyes and answered Chamu Khan's questions regarding his people and his country with patience. He wondered at the absurdity of most of these questions, and at the emperor's evident ignorance and stupidity. Old Roogla, the general, a fiercely mustached, barrel-chested savage, was present and he said nothing. But his eyes strayed in comparison from the fat, helpless mass of flesh and arrogance on the cushions to the erect, broad-shouldered figure and hard, scarred face of the Frank. From the corner of his eye Chamu Khan observed this but he was not altogether a fool. He spoke pleasantly to Godric, but the wary Norman, used to dealing with rulers, sensed that dislike was mixed with the khan's feeling of obligation, and that this dislike was mingled with fear. Chamu asked him suddenly of Genghis Khan and watched him narrowly. The sincerity of the knight's reply evidently convinced Chamu, for a shadow of relief passed over his fat face. After all, decided Godric, it was but natural that an emperor should be suspicious of a stranger in his realm, especially one of such war-like aspects as the Norman knew himself to be.

At the end of the interview, Chamu fastened a heavy golden chain about Godric's neck with his own pudgy hands. Then Godric went back to his chamber with the lapis lazuli dome, to the cherry blossoms drifting in gay-colored clouds from the breeze-shaken trees, and to lazy strolls and talks with Yulita.

"It seems strange," said he abruptly one day, "that you are to leave this land and go to another. Somehow I can not think of you save as a slim girl forever under these blossom-heavy trees, with the dreamy fountains singing and the mountains of Black Cathay rising against the skies."

She caught her breath and turned away her face as if from an inner hurt.

"There are cherry trees in Cathay," said she, without looking at him, "and fountains too -- and finer palaces than I have ever seen."

"But there are no such mountains," returned the knight.

"No," her voice was low, "there are no such mountains -- nor -- "

"Nor what?"

"No Frankish knight to save me from bandits," she laughed suddenly and gayly.

"Nor will there be here, long," he said somberly. "The time approaches when I must take the trail again. I come of a restless breed and I have dallied here overlong."

"Whither will you go, oh Godric?" Did she catch her breath suddenly as she spoke?

"Who knows?" In his voice was the ancient bitterness that his heathen Viking ancestors knew. "The world is before me -- but not all the world with its shining leagues of sea or sand can quench the hunger that is in me. I must ride -- that is all I know. I must ride till the ravens pluck my bones. Perchance I will ride back to tell Montferrat that his dream of an Eastern empire is a bubble that has burst. Perhaps I will ride east again."

"Not east," she shook her head. "The ravens are gathering in the east and there is a red flame there that pales the night. Wang Khan and his Keraits have fallen before the riders of Genghis Khan and Hia reels before his onslaught. Black Cathay too, I fear, is doomed, unless the Chins send them aid."

"Would you care if I fell?" he asked curiously.

Her clear eyes surveyed him.

"Would I care? I would care if a dog died. Surely then I would care if a man who saved my life, fell."

He shrugged his mighty shoulders. "You are kind. Today I ride. My wounds are long healed. I can lift my sword again. Thanks to your care I am strong as I ever was. This has been paradise -- but I come of a restless breed. My dream of a kingdom is shattered and I must ride -- somewhere. I have heard much from the slaves and You-tai of this Genghis Khan and his chiefs. Aye, of Subotai and Chepe Noyon. I will lend my sword to him -- "

"And fight against my people?" she asked.

His gaze fell before her clear eyes. "'Twere the deed of a dog," he muttered. "But what would you have? I am a soldier -- I have fought for and against the same men since I rode east. A warrior must pick the winning side. And Genghis Khan, from all accounts, is a born conqueror."

Her eyes flashed. "The Cathayans will send out an army and crush him. He can not take Jahadur -- what do his skin-clad herders know of walled cities?"

"We were but a naked horde before Constantinople," muttered Godric, "but we had hunger to drive us on and the city fell. Genghis and his men are hungry. I have seen men of the same breed. Your people are fat and indolent. Genghis Khan will ride them down like sheep."

"And you will aid him," she blazed.

"War is a man's game," he said roughly; shame hardened his tone; this slim, clear-eyed girl, so ignorant and innocent of the world's ways, stirred old dreams of idealistic chivalry in his soul -- dreams he thought long lost in the fierce necessity of life. "What do you know of war and men's perfidy? A warrior must better himself as he may. I am weary of fighting for lost causes and getting only hard blows in return."

"What if I asked you -- begged you?" she breathed, leaning forward.

A sudden surge of madness swept him off his feet.

"For you," he roared suddenly, like a wounded lion, "I would ride down on the Mongol yurts alone and crush them into the red earth and bring back the heads of Genghis and his khans in a cluster at my saddle-bow!"

She recoiled, gasping before the sudden loosing of his passion, but he caught her in an unconsciously rough embrace. His race loved as they hated, fiercely and violently. He would not have bruised her tender skin for all the gold in Cathay, but his own savagery swept him out of himself.

Then a sudden voice brought him to himself and he released the girl and whirled, ready to battle the whole Black Cathayan army. Old Roogla stood before them, panting.

"My princess," he gasped; "the courtiers from Greater Cathay -- they have just arrived -- "

She went white and cold as a statue.

"I am ready, oh Roogla," she whispered.

"Ready the devil!" roared the old soldier. "Only three of them got through to the gates of Jahadur and they're bleeding to death! You are not going to Cathay to marry Wang Yin. Not now, at least. And you'll be lucky if you're not dragged by the hair to Subotai's yurt. The hills are swarming with Mongols. They cut the throats of the watchers in the passes, and ambushed the courtiers from Cathay. An hour will bring them -- the whole horde of howling devils -- to the very gates of Jahadur. Chamu Khan is capering about like a devil with a hornet in his khalat. We can't send you out now -- Genghis holds all the outer passes. The western Turks might give you sanctuary -- but we can not reach them. There's only one thing to do -- and that's hold the city! But with these fat, perfume-scented, wine-bibbing dogs that call themselves soldiery we'll be lucky if we get to strike a single blow in our defense -- "

Yulita turned to Godric with level eyes.

"Genghis Khan is at our gates," said she. "Go to him." And turning she walked swiftly into a nearby doorway.

"What did she mean?" asked old Roogla wonderingly.

Godric growled deep in his throat. "Bring my armor and my sword. I go to seek Genghis Khan -- but not as she thought."

Roogla grinned and his beard bristled. He smote Godric a blow that had rendered a lesser man senseless.

"Hai, wolf-brother!" he roared; "we'll give Genghis a fight yet! We'll send him back to the desert to lick his wounds if we can only keep three men in the army from fleeing! They can stand behind us and hand us weapons when we break our swords and axes, while we pile up Mongol dead so high that the women on the battlements will look up at them!" Godric smiled thinly.

CHAPTER III

"To grow old cowed in a conquered land,
With the sun itself discrowned,
To see trees crouch and cattle slink --
Death is a better ale to drink,
And by high Death on the fell brink,
That flagon shall go round."

-- Chesterton

Godric's armor had been mended cleverly, he found, the rents in hauberk and helmet fused with such skill that no sign of a gash showed. The knight's armor was unusually strong, anyway, and of a weight few men could have borne. The blades that had wounded him in the battle of the defiles had hacked through old dents. Now that these were mended, the armor was like new. The heavy mail was reinforced with solid plates of steel on breast, back and shoulders and the sword belt was of joined steel plates a hand's breadth wide. The helmet, instead of being merely a steel cap with a long nasal, worn over a mail hood, as was the case of most Crusaders, was made with a vizor and fitted firmly into the steel shoulder-pieces. The whole armor showed the trend of the times -- chain and scale mail giving way gradually to plate armor.

Godric experienced a fierce resurge of power as he felt the familiar weight of his mail and fingered the worn hilt of his long, two-handed sword. The languorous illusive dreaminess of the past weeks vanished; again he was a conqueror of a race of conquerors. With old Roogla he rode to the main gates, seeing on all hands the terror that had seized the people. Men and women ran distractedly through the streets, crying that the Mongols were upon them; they tied their belongings into bundles, loaded them on donkeys and jerked them off again, shouting reproaches at the soldiers on the walls, who seemed as frightened as the people.

"Cowards!" old Roogla's beard bristled. "What they need is war to stiffen their thews. Well, they've got war now and they'll have to fight."

"A man can always run," answered Godric sardonically.

They came to the outer gates and found a band of soldiery there, handling their pikes and bows nervously. They brightened slightly as Roogla and Godric rode up. The tale of the Norman's battle with the Hian bandits had lost nothing in the telling. But Godric was surprised to note their fewness.

"Are these all your soldiers?"

Roogla shook his head.

"Most of them are at the Pass of Skulls," he growled. "It's the only way a large force of men can approach Jahadur. In the past we've held it easily against all comers -- but these Mongols are devils. I left enough men here to hold the city against any stray troops that might climb down the cliffs."

They rode out of the gates and down the winding mountain trail. On one side rose a sheer wall, a thousand feet high. On the other side the cliff fell away three times that distance into a fathomless chasm. A mile's ride brought them to the Pass of Skulls. Here the trail debouched into a sort of upland plateau, passing between two walls of sheer rock.

A thousand warriors were encamped there, gaudy in their silvered mail, long-toed leather boots and gold-chased weapons. With their peaked helmets with mail drops, their long spears and wide-bladed scimitars, they seemed war-like enough. They were big men, but they were evidently nervous and uncertain.

"By the blood of the devil, Roogla," snapped Godric, "have you no more soldiers than these?"

"Most of the troops are scattered throughout the empire," Roogla answered. "I warned Chamu Khan to collect all the warriors in the empire here, but he refused to do so. Why, Erlik alone knows. Well, a man can always die."

He rose in his saddle and his great voice roared through the hills: "Men of Black Cathay, you know me of old! But here beside me is one you know only by word of mouth; a chief out of the West who will fight beside you today. Now take heart, and when Genghis comes up the defile, show him Black Cathayans can still die like men!"

"Not so fast," growled Godric. "This pass looks impregnable to me. May I have a word as to the arranging of the troops?"

Roogla spread his hands. "Assuredly."

"Then set men to work rebuilding that barricade," snapped Godric, pointing to the wavering lines of stone, half tumbled down, which spanned the pass.

"Build it high and block that gate. There'll be no caravans passing through today. I thought you were a soldier; it should have been done long ago. Put your best bowmen behind the first line of stone. Then the spearmen, and the swordsmen and ax-fighters behind the spearmen -- "

The long hot day wore on. At last far away sounded the deep rattle of many kettledrums, then a thunder of myriad hoofs. Then up the deep defile and out onto the plateau swept a bizarre and terrible horde. Godric had expected a wild, motley mass of barbarians, like a swarm of locusts without order or system. These men rode in compact formation, of such as he had never before seen; in well ordered ranks, divided into troops of a thousand each.

The tugh, the yak-tail standards, were lifted above them. At the sight of their orderly array and hard-bitten appearance, Godric's heart sank. These men were used to fierce warfare; they outnumbered his own soldiers by seven times. How could he hope to hold the pass against them even for a little while? Godric swore deeply and fervently and put the hope of survival from him; thereafter during the whole savage fight, his one idea was to do as much damage to the enemy as he possibly could before he died.

Now he stood on the first line of fortifications and gazed curiously at the advancing hosts, seeing stocky, broad-built men mounted on wiry horses, men with square flat faces, devoid of humor or mercy, whose armor was plain stuff of hardened leather, lacquer, or iron plates laced together. With a wry face he noted the short, heavy bows and long arrows. From the look of those bows he knew they would drive shafts through ordinary mail as if it were paper. Their other weapons consisted of spears, short-handled axes, maces and curved sabers, lighter and more easily handled than the huge two-handed scimitars of the Black Cathayans.

Roogla, standing at his shoulder, pointed to a giant riding ahead of the army.

"Subotai," he growled, "a Uriankhi -- from the frozen tundras, with a heart as cold as his native land. He can twist a spear shaft in two between his hands. The tall fop riding beside him is Chepe Noyon; note his silvered mail and heron plumes. And by Erlik, there is Kassar the Strong, sword-bearer to the khan. Well -- if Genghis himself is not here now, he soon will be, for he never allows Kassar long out of his sight -- the Strong One is a fool, useful only in actual combat."

Godric's cold gray eyes were fixed on the giant form of Subotai; a growing fury stirred in him, not a tangible hatred of the Uriankhi but the fighting rage one strong man feels when confronted by a foe his equal in prowess. The knight expected a parley but evidently the Mongols were of a different mind. They came sweeping across the boulder-strewn plateau like a wind from Hell, a swarm of mounted bowmen preceding them.

"Down!" roared Godric, as shafts began to rain around him. "Down behind the rocks! Spearmen and swordsmen lie flat! Archers return their fire."

Roogla repeated the shout and arrows began to fly from the barricades. But the effort was half-hearted. The sight of that onrushing horde had numbed the men of Jahadur. Godric had never seen men ride and shoot from the saddle as these Mongols did. They were barely within arrow flight, yet men were falling along the lines of stone. He felt the Jahadurans wavering -- realized with a flood of blind rage that they would break before the Mongol heavy cavalry reached the barricade. A bowman near him roared and fell backward with an arrow through his throat and a shout went up from the faltering Black Cathayans.

"Fools!" raged Godric, smiting right and left with clenched fists. "Horsemen can never take this pass if you stand to it! Bend your bows and throw your shoulders into it! Fight, damn you!"

The bowmen had split to either side, and through the gap the flying swordsmen swept. Now if ever was the time to break the charge, but the Jahaduran bowmen loosed wildly or not at all and behind them the spearmen were scrambling up to flee. Old Roogla was screaming and tearing his hair, cursing the day he was born, and not a man had fallen on the Mongols' side. Even at that distance Godric, standing upright on the barricade, saw the broad grin on Subotai's face. With a bitter curse he tore a spear from the hand of a warrior near by and threw every ounce of his mighty-thewed frame into the cast.

It was too far for an ordinary spearcast even to carry -- but with a hum the spear hissed through the air and the Mongol next to Subotai fell headlong, transfixed. From the Black Cathayan ranks rose a sudden roar. These riders could be slain after all! And surely no mortal man could have made that cast! Godric, towering above them on the barricade, like a man of iron, suddenly assumed supernatural proportions in the eyes of the warriors behind him. How could they be defeated when such a man led them? The quick fire of Oriental battle-lust blazed up and sudden courage surged through the veins of the wavering warriors.

With a shout they pulled shaft to ear and loosed, and a sudden hail of death smote the charging Mongols. At that range there was no missing. Those long shafts tore through buckler and hauberk, transfixing the wearers. Flesh and blood could not stand it. The charge did not exactly break, but in the teeth of that iron gale the squadrons wheeled and circled away out of range. A wild yell of triumph rose from the Jahadurans and they waved their spears and shouted taunts.

Old Roogla was in ecstasies, but Godric snarled a mirthless laugh. At least he had whipped courage into the Black Cathayans. But here, he knew, he and Roogla and all the others would leave their corpses before the day was over. And Yulita -- he would not allow himself to think of her. At least, he swore, a red mist waving in front of his eyes, Subotai would not take her.

The yak tails were waving, the kettledrums beating for another charge. This time the bowmen rode out more warily, loosing a perfect rain of shafts. At Godric's order his men did not return the fire, but sheltered themselves behind their barricade; he himself stood contemptuously upright, trusting to the strength of his half-plate armor. He became the center of the fire, but the long shafts glanced harmlessly from his shield or splintered on his hauberk.

The horsemen wheeled closer, drawing harder on their heavy bows, and at Godric's word the Jahadurans answered them. In a short fierce exchange the men in the open had the worst of it. They galloped out of range with several empty saddles, but Godric had not let his attention stray from the real menace -- the heavily armed cavalry. These had approached at a rapid trot while the arrow fire was being exchanged, and now they struck in the spurs and came like a bolt from a crossbow.

Again the sweeping rain of arrows met and broke them, though this time their momentum carried them to within a hundred feet of the barricades. One rider broke through to the lines and Godric saw a wild figure, spurting blood and hewing madly at him. Then as the Mongol rose in his stirrups to reach the knight's head, a dozen spears, thrusting over the backs of the bowmen, pierced him and hurled him headlong.

Again the Mongols retreated out of range, but this time their losses had been severe. Riderless horses ranged the plateau, which was dotted with still or writhing forms.

Already the Jahadurans had inflicted more damage on the men of Genghis Khan than the Mongols were accustomed to. But from the way the nomads ranged themselves for the third charge, Godric knew that this time no flight of arrows would stop them. He spared a moment's admiration for their courage.

The supply of arrows was running low. Black Cathay, as in all things pertaining to war, had neglected the manufacture of war-arrows. A large number of shafts remaining in the quivers of the archers were hunting-arrows, good only at short range.

This time there was no great exchange between the bowmen. The archers of Subotai mingled themselves among the front ranks of the swordsmen, and when the charge came, a sheet of arrows preceded it.

"Save your shafts!" roared Godric, gripping the ax he had chosen from the arms of Jahadur. "Back, archers -- spearmen, on the wall!"

The next moment the headlong horde broke like a red wave on the barricade. Evidently they had misjudged the strength of those stone lines, not knowing them newly reinforced -- had expected to shatter them by sheer weight and velocity and to ride through the ruins. But the strengthened walls held.

Horses hit the barricade with a splintering of bones, and men's brains were dashed out by the shock. Doubtless they had expected to sacrifice the first line, but the slaughter was greater than they could have reckoned. The second line, hot on the heels of the first, plunged against the wall over its writhing remnants, and the third line piled up on both. The whole line of the barricade was a red welter of dying, screaming horses, lashing hoofs and writhing men, while the blood-maddened Jahadurans yelled like wolves, hacking and stabbing down at the crimson shambles.

The rear lines ruthlessly trampled down their dying comrades to strike at the defenders, but the ground was thick with dead and wounded and the plunging, writhing horses fouled the hoofs that swept over them. Still, some of the Mongols did gain through to the lines and made a desperate effort to clamber over the wall. They died like rats in a trap beneath the lunging spears of the inspired Black Cathayans.

One, a huge brutal-faced giant, rode over a writhing welter of red torn flesh, reined in close to the barricade and an iron mace in his hands dashed out the brains of a spearman. From both hosts rose a shout of: "Kassar!"

"Kassar, eh?" growled Godric, stepping forward on the precarious top of the barricade. The giant rose in his stirrups, the clotted mace swung back and at that instant the twenty-pound battle-ax in Godric's right hand crashed down on the peaked helmet. Ax and helmet shattered together and the steed went to his knees under the shock. Then it reared and plunged wildly away, Kassar's crumpled body lolling and swaying in the saddle, held by the deep stirrups.

Godric tossed away the splintered ax-haft and picked up the mace that had fallen on the stones. He heard old Roogla shouting: "Bogda! Bogda! Bogda! Gurgaslan!"

The whole host of Jahadur took up the shout; thus Godric gained his new name, which means the Lion, and crimson was the christening.

The Mongols were again in slow, stubborn retreat and Godric brandished the mace and shouted: "Ye be men! Stand to it boldly! Already have you slain more than half your own number!"

But he knew that now the real death grip was about to be. The Mongols were dismounting. Horsemen by nature and choice, they had realized however that cavalry charges could never take those solid walls, manned by inspired madmen. They held their round, lacquered bucklers before them and swung solidly onward in much the same formation as they had maintained mounted.

They rolled like a black tide over the corpse-strewn plain and like a black flood they burst on the spear-bristling wall. Few arrows were loosed on either side. The Black Cathayans had emptied their quivers and the Mongols wished only to come to hand-grips.

The line of barricades became a red line of Hell. Spears jabbed downward, curved blades broke on lances. In the very teeth of the girding steel, the Mongols strove to climb the wall, piling heaps of their own dead for grim ladders. Most of them were pierced by the spears of the defenders, and the few who did win over the barriers were cut down by the swordsmen behind the spearmen.

The nomads perforce fell back a few yards, then surged on again. The terrific shocks of their impact shook the whole barricade. These men needed no shouts or commands to spur them on. They were fired with an indomitable will which emanated from within as well as from without. Godric saw Chepe Noyon fighting silently on foot with the rest of the warriors. Subotai sat his horse a few yards back of the mass, directing the movements.

Charge after charge crashed against the barriers. The Mongols were wasting lives like water and Godric wondered at their unquenchable resolve to conquer this relatively unimportant mountain kingdom. But he realized that Genghis Khan's whole future as a conqueror depended on his stamping out all opposition, no matter what the cost.

The wall was crumbling. The Mongols were tearing it to pieces. They could not climb it, so they thrust their spears between the stones and loosened them, tearing them away with bare hands. They died as they toiled, but their comrades trampled their corpses and took up their work.

Subotai leaped from his horse, snatched a heavy curved sword from his saddle and joined the warriors on foot. He gained to the center of the wall and tore at it with his naked hands, disdaining the down-lunging spears which broke on his helmet and armor. A breach was made and the Mongols began to surge through.

Godric yelled fiercely and leaped to stem the sudden tide, but a wash of the black wave over the wall hemmed him in with howling fiends. A crashing sweep of his mace cleared a red way and he plunged through. The Mongols were coming over the ruins of the barriers and through the great breach Subotai had made. Godric shouted for the Jahadurans to fall back, and even as he did, he saw Roogla parrying the whistling strokes of Chepe Noyon's curved scimitar.

The old general was bleeding already from a deep gash in the thigh, and even as the Norman sprang to aid him, the Mongol's blade cut through Roogla's mail and blood spurted. Roogla slumped slowly to the earth and Chepe Noyon wheeled to meet the knight's furious charge. He flung up his sword to parry the whistling mace, but the giant Norman in his berserk rage dealt a blow that made nothing of skill or tempered steel. The scimitar flew to singing sparks, the helmet cracked and Chepe Noyon was dashed to earth like a pole-axed steer.

"Bear Roogla back!" roared Godric, leaping forward and swinging his mace up again to dash out the prostrate Mongol's brains as a man kills a wounded snake. But even as the mace crashed downward, a squat warrior leaped like a panther, arms wide, shielding the fallen chieftain's body with his own and taking the stroke on his own head. His shattered corpse fell across Chepe Noyon and a sudden determined rush of Mongols bore Godric back. Even as the Jahadurans bore the desperately wounded Roogla back across the next line of stone, the Mongols lifted the stunned Chepe Noyon and carried him out of the battle.

Fighting stubbornly, Godric retreated, half-ringed by the squat shapes that fought so silently and thrust so fiercely for his life. He reached the next wall, over which the Jahadurans had already gone, and for a moment stood at bay, back against the stones, while spears flashed at him and curved sabers hacked at him. His armor had saved him thus far, though a shrewd thrust had girded deep into the calf of his leg and a heavy blow on his hauberk had partly numbed the shoulder beneath.

Now the Black Cathayans leaned over the wall, cleared a space with their spears and seizing their champion under the armpits, lifted him bodily over. The fight rolled on. Life became to the men on the walls one red continuance of hurtling bodies and lunging blades. The spears of the defenders were bent or splintered. The arrows were gone. Half the Black Cathayans were dead. Most of the rest were wounded. But possessed of a fanatical fervor they fought on, swinging their notched axes and blunted scimitars as fiercely as if the fight had but started. The full fighting fury of their Turkish ancestors was roused and only death could quench it. After all, they were of the same blood as these unconquerable demons from the Gobi.

The second barricade crumbled and the Jahadurans began to fall back to the last line of barricades. But this time the Mongols were over the falling stones and upon them before they could make good their escape. Godric and fifty men, covering the withdrawal of the rest, were cut off. Then the others would have come back over the wall to aid them, but a solid mass of Mongols were between that balked their fiercest efforts.

Godric's men died about him like hunted wolves, slaying and dying without a groan or whimper. Their last gasps were snarls of deathless fury. Their heavy two-handed scimitars wrought fearful destruction among their stocky foes but the Mongols ran in under the sweep of the blades and ripped upward with their shorter sabers.

Godric's plated mail saved him from chance blows and his enormous strength and amazing quickness made him all but invincible. His shield he had long discarded. He gripped the heavy mace in both hands and it smashed like a black god of death through the battle rout. Blood and brains splashed like water as shields, helmets and corselets gave way. Across the heads of the hacking warriors Godric saw the giant frame of Subotai, looming head and shoulders above his men. With a curse the Norman hurled the mace, which spattered blood as it hummed through the air. Men cried out at the long cast, but Subotai ducked swiftly. Godric whipped out his two-handed sword for the first time during the fight, and the long straight blade which the Pope had blessed years ago shimmered like a living thing -- like the blue waves of the western sea.

It was a heavy blade, forged to cut through thick mail and strong plates, armor many times heavier than that worn by most Orientals, who usually preferred shirts of light chain mail. Godric wielded it in one hand as lightly as most men could swing it with both. His left hand held a dirk, point upward, and they who ducked beneath the sword to grapple, died from the thrust of the shorter blade. The Norman set his back against a heap of dead, and in a red haze of battle madness, split skulls to the teeth, cleft bosoms to the spine, severed shoulder bones, hewed through neck cords, hacked off legs at the hip and arms at the shoulder until they gave back in sudden, unaccustomed fear and stood panting and eyeing him as hunters eye a wounded tiger.

And Godric laughed at them, taunted them, spat in their faces. Centuries of civilizing French influence were wiped away; it was a berserk Viking who faced his paling foes.

He was wounded, he faintly sensed, but unweakened. The fire of fury left no room in his brain for any other sensation. A giant form surged through the ranks, flinging men right and left as spray is flung by a charging galley. Subotai of the frozen tundras stood before his foe at last.

Godric took in the height of the man, the mighty sweep of chest and shoulder, and the massive arms which wielded the sword that had more than once, during the fight, sheared clear through the torso of a mailed Jahaduran.

"Back!" roared Subotai, his fierce eyes alight -- those eyes were blue, Godric noted, and the Mongol's hair red; surely somewhere in that frozen land of tundras a wandering Aryan strain had mingled with the Turanian blood of Subotai's tribe -- "Back, and give us room! None shall slay this chief but Subotai!"

Somewhere down the deep defile there sounded a rally of kettledrums and the tramp of many hoofs, but Godric was hardly aware he heard. He saw the Mongols fall back, leaving a space clear. He heard Chepe Noyon, still slightly groggy, and with a new helmet, shouting orders at the men who surged about the wall. Fighting ceased altogether and all eyes turned on the chiefs, who swung up their blades and rushed together like two maddened bulls.

Godric knew that his armor would never stand against the full sweep of the great sword Subotai was swinging in his right hand. The Norman leaped and struck as a tiger strikes, throwing every ounce of his body behind the blow and nerving himself to superhuman quickness. His heavy, straight blade sheared through the lacquered buckler Subotai flung above his head, and crashing full on the peaked helmet, bit through to the scalp beneath. Subotai staggered, a jet of blood trickling down his dark face, but almost instantly swung a decapitating stroke that whistled harmlessly through the air as Godric bent his knees quickly. The Frank thrust viciously but Subotai evaded the lunging point with a twist of his huge frame and hacked in savagely. Godric sprang away but could not entirely avoid the blow. The great blade struck under his armpit, crunched through the mail and bit deep into his ribs. The impact numbed his whole left side, and in an instant his hauberk was full of blood.

Stung to renewed madness, Godric sprang in, parrying the scimitar, then dropped his sword and grappled Subotai. The Mongol returned the fierce embrace, drawing a dagger. Close-locked they wrestled and strained, staggering on hard-braced legs, each seeking to break the other's spine or to drive home his own blade. Both weapons were reddened in an instant as they girded through the crevices in the armor or were driven straight through solid mail, but neither could free his hand enough to drive in a death thrust.

Godric was gasping for breath; he felt that the pressure of the Mongol's huge arms was crushing him. But Subotai was in no better way. The Norman saw sweat thickly beading the Mongol's brow, heard his breath coming in heavy pants, and a savage joy shook him.

Subotai lifted his foe bodily to dash him headlong, but Godric's grip held them together so firmly this was impossible. With both feet braced on the blood-soaked earth again, Godric suddenly ceased trying to free his dirk wrist from Subotai's iron grip, and releasing the Mongol's dagger arm, drove his left fist into Subotai's face.

With the full power of mighty arm and broad shoulders behind it, the blow was like that of a club. Blood spattered and Subotai's head snapped back as if on hinges -- but at that instant he drove his dagger deep in Godric's breast muscles.

The Norman gasped, staggered, and then in a last burst of strength he flung the Mongol from him. Subotai fell his full length and rose slowly, dazedly, like a man who has fought out the last red ounce of his endurance. His mighty frame sagged back on the arms of the ringing warriors and he shook his head like a bull, striving to nerve himself again for the combat.

Godric recovered the sword he had dropped and now he faced his foes, feet braced wide against his sick dizziness. He groped a moment for support and felt firm stones at his back. The fight had carried them almost to the last barricades. There he faced the Mongols like a wounded lion at bay, head lowered on his mighty, mailed breast, terrible eyes glittering through the bars of his vizor, both hands gripping his red sword.

"Come on," he challenged as he felt his life waning in thick red surges. "Mayhap I die -- but I will slay seven of you before I die. Come in and make an ending, you pagan swine!"

Men thronged the plateau behind the tattered horde -- thousands of them. A powerful, bearded chieftain on a white horse rode forward and surveyed the silent, battle-weary Mongols and the stone bulwark with its thin ranks of bloody defenders. This, Godric knew in a weary way, was the great Genghis Khan and he wished he had enough life left in him to charge through the ranks and hew the khan from his saddle; but weakness began to steal over him.

"A good thing I came with the Horde," said Genghis Khan sardonically. "It seems these Cathayans have been drinking some wine that makes men of them. They have slain more Mongols already than the Keraits and the Hians did. Who spurred these scented women to battle?"

"He." Chepe Noyon pointed to the bloodstained knight. "By Erlik, they have drunk blood this day. The Frank is a devil; my head still sings from the blow he dealt me; Kassar is but now recovering his senses from an ax the Frank shattered on his helmet, and he has but now fought Subotai himself to a standstill."

Genghis reigned his horse forward and Godric tensed himself. If the khan would only come within reach -- a sudden spring, a last, desperate blow -- if he could but take this paynim lord with him to the realm of death, he would die content.

The great, deep gray eyes of Genghis were upon the knight and he felt their full power.

"You are of such steel as my chiefs are forged from," said Genghis. "I would have you for friend, not foe. You are not of the race of those men; come and serve under me."

"My ears are dull with blows on my helmet," answered Godric, tightening his grip on his hilt and tensing his weary muscles; "I can not understand you. Come closer that I may hear you."

Instead Genghis reigned his steed back a few paces and grinned with tolerant understanding.

"Will you serve me?" he persisted. "I will make you a chief."

"And what of these?" Godric indicated the Black Cathayans.

Genghis shrugged his shoulders. "What am I to do with them? They must die."

"Go to your brother the Devil," Godric growled. "I come of a race that sell their swords for gold -- but we are no jackals to turn on men that have bled beside us. These warriors and I have already killed more than our own number and wounded many more of your warriors. There are still three hundred of us left and the strongest of the barricades. We have slain over a thousand of your wolves -- if you enter Jahadur you ride over our corpses. Charge in now and see how desperate men can die."

"But you owe no allegiance to Jahadur," argued Genghis.

"I owe my life to Chamu Khan," snapped Godric. "I have thrown in my lot with him and I serve him with as much fealty as if he were the Pope himself."

"You are a fool," Genghis said frankly. "I have long had my spies among the Jahadurans. Chamu planned to sacrifice Jahadur and all therein to save his own hide. That is why he refused to bring more soldiers to the city. His main force he gathered on the western border. He planned to flee by a secret way through the cliffs as soon as I attacked the pass.

"Well, he did, but some of my warriors came upon him. They only asked a gift of him," Genghis chuckled. "Then they made no effort to hinder him. He might then go where he would. Would you see the gift they took from Chamu Khan?"

And a Mongol behind the khan held up a ghastly, grinning head. Godric cursed: "Liar, traitor and coward though he was, he was yet a king. Come in and make an ending. I swear to you that before you ride over this wall, your horses will tread fetlock-deep in a carpet of your dead."

Still Genghis sat his horse and pondered. Subotai came up to him, and grinning broadly, spoke in his ear. The Khan nodded.

"Swear to serve me and I will spare the lives of your men; I will take Black Cathay unharmed into my empire."

Godric turned to his men. "You heard -- I would rather die here on a heap of Mongol dead -- but it is for you to say."

They answered with a shout: "The emperor is dead! Why should we die, if Genghis Khan will grant us peace? Give us Gurgaslan for ruler and we will serve you."

Genghis raised his hand. "So be it!"

Godric shook the blood and sweat out of his eyes and snarled a bitter laugh.

"A puppet king on a tinsel throne, to dance on your string, Mongol? No! Get another for the task."

Genghis scowled and suddenly swore. "By the yellow face of Erlik! I have already made more concessions today than I ever made in my life before! What want ye, Gurgaslan -- shall I give you my scepter for a war-club?"

"If he wishes it you may as well give it to him," grinned Subotai, who was no more awed by his khan than if Genghis had been a horse-boy. "These Franks are built of iron without and within. Reason with him, Genghis!"

The khan glared at his general for a moment as if he were of a mind to brain him, then grinned suddenly. These men of the steppes were a frank, open race greatly different from the devious-minded peoples of Asia Minor.

"To have you and your warriors fighting beside me," said Genghis calmly, "I will do that which I never expected to do. You are fit to tread the crimson road of empire. Take Black Cathay and rule it as you will; I ask only that you aid me in my wars, as an equal ally. We will be two kings, reigning side by side and aiding each other against all enemies."

Godric's thin lips smiled. "It is fair enough."

The Mongols sent up a thunderous roar and the bloody Jahadurans swarmed over the barricades to kiss the hands of their new ruler. He did not hear Genghis say to the warrior who bore the grisly severed head of Chamu Khan: "See that the skull is prepared and sheathed in silver, and set among the rest that were khans of tribes; when I fall I would wish my own skull treated with the same respect."

Godric felt a firm grasp on his hand and looked into the steady eyes of Subotai, feeling a rush of friendship for the man that equaled his former rage.

"Erlik, what a man!" growled the chief. "We should be good comrades, Gurgaslan! Here -- by the gods, man, you are sorely wounded! He swoons -- get off his armor and see to his hurts, you thick-headed fools, do you want him to die?"

"Scant chance," grinned Chepe Noyon, feeling his head tenderly. "Such men as he are not made to die from steel. Wait, you big buffalo, you'll kill him with your clumsiness. I'll bring one more fitted to attend him -- one that was found being forcibly escorted out of Jahadur by the palace eunuchs. I saw her only five minutes agone and I am almost ready to cut your throat for her, Gurgaslan. Genghis, will you bid them bring the girl?"

Again Godric saw, as in a closing mist, two great dark eyes bend over him -- he felt soft arms go about his neck and heard a sobbing in his ear.

"Well, Yulita," he said as in a dream, "I went to Genghis Khan after all!"

"You saved Black Cathay, my king," she sobbed, pressing her lips against his. Then while his dull head swam those soft lips were withdrawn and a goblet took their place, filled with a stinging wine that jerked him back into consciousness.

Genghis was standing over him.

"You have already found your queen, eh?" he smiled. "Well -- rest of your wounds; I will not need your aid for some months yet. Marry your queen, organize your kingdom -- there is a great army drawn up on the western border ready to your hand now that there is to be no invasion of your kingdom. It may be the western Turks will dispute your liegeship -- you have but to send the word and I will send you as many riders as you need. When the desert grass deepens for spring, we ride in to Greater Cathay."

The khan turned on his heel and strode away and Godric gathered the slim form of Yulita into his weary arms.

"Wang Yin will wait long for his bride," said he, and the laughter of Yulita was like the tinkle of the silvery fountains in the cherry blossom courts of Jahadur. And so the dream that had haunted Godric de Villehard of an Eastern empire woke to life.